The Fork with The Scales

A Magic Shop Fantasy Short Story

for me

The Fork with The Scales

A Magic Shop Fantasy Short Story

TOPAZ HAUYN

Visit us online:
www.topazhauyn.com

ISBN: 9798794986334
Font: Alegreya
Coverdesign: Topaz Hauyn
Art: grandfailure/depositphotos.com

Amanda of the Hidden Unknown sat in her wooden rocking chair that squeaked with each swing. The squeaking and cracking of the wood under her small weight was the perfect background sound for her business. Nobody came into her tea shop to drink tea out of white, perfect cups and eat a piece off of perfectly designed cake in here.

Her business was different. Customers got their tea or hot chocolate in a myriad of different cups.

She had collected them from all time periods, places and customers, for she didn't take money for her food. Who ever wants to get some paper with colors printed on or some metal or plastic chips with heads and symbols of states and kingdoms that did last a bit longer or a bit shorter?

Others might.

She didn't.

Instead, she accepted rare cups. Rare defined as, not in her vast collection presented yet on the small shelves that ran around all the walls. She also accepted plates, forks and spoons which were equally rare, meaning not on any of the shelves in the respective rooms. A collection she didn't use as a museum, like her parents had once told her to do.

May the God of Hiding and the Goodness of the Unknown forbid. No, she used her treasury. Presented her collection to every customer. Even more, every customer had to choose the cup and plate for his tea or her cake from the many shelves. One from the room of cups, one from the room of plates, one from the room of forks and spoons.

The thing Amanda loved the most in her business was watching her customers look at all the cups in the first room, then all the plates in the second room. Most searched for a perfect match. Something that was rarely found. But they made up stories to cover up for that lack.

While she placed the cake on the plate and cooked the water of the tea, they explained why a certain cup fit perfectly with a certain plate, not knowing they gave their identity and their core beliefs away doing so.

Easy customers. Nice days. Full of stories, she collected in her story book in the back-office.

Usually in the evening, she wrote down those that stuck out during the day.

For that she sat at her large desk in the back-office, next to the window that went out north, with the company of her fairy friend Princess and dragon pet.

Only that today, no customer had shown up.

Not a single one.

Amanda of the Hidden Unknown didn't know what was wrong.

Usually customers trickled in from the various doors she had into the human world by the time she finished baking the first cake for the day. They stepped in through her front door. Some dusted off their clothes, others stomped snow from their boots, most looked like they had just walked by on a street in front of the house.

Today, the whole cake table was full. She had scrubbed the kitchen clean and sat, dressed in a fresh, red dress with frills at the hem, in her rocking chair in the first room.

Waiting.

Watching her cup collection and wondering what might have happened.

All tables were set. Little square ones, with one or two chairs each, for the occasional couple. Today with red tablecloth, fitting her dress.

Yesterday had been a long day.

The last customer had come shortly before she closed the door for the day. He took the first cup, in the upmost row. One made of tin with small, triangle shaped patterns all around. He wore a long cape, like adventurers usually did. So long it swiped over the wooden floor when he stepped into the second room. There he had also chosen the first plate from the upmost row of shelves. He repeated that process with the spoons, the forks and the cakes.

Always taking the first.

Worse: He didn't come up with a story why those things fit together.

He had paid with a fork which was formed from a snake with three heads. The body the handle, the heads the three tips of the fork. The color was green. Might be colored, might be a special crystal, might be a metal mix.

Amanda of the Hidden Unknown didn't know and usually didn't care.

Why did she question the material yesterday? Maybe because the customer didn't offer a story?

Usually, she could use the story to trace back the history of her new item. Her house listened as well. And when she added the new inventory into her large books, the stories of the items appeared below her writing.

She had accepted the fork and put it into her collection with the other greenish forks.

»Put it first place on the upmost shelf«, had the customer said, still standing in the room with his plate and steaming cup of cherry tea. His raspy voice had sent a shiver over her forearms. Not because of the sound, but because of the idea, that he could decide where she placed the fork.

Amanda still felt the annoyance of that voice. The hairs on her forearms stood up. Even under the tight-fitting sleeves of her red dress.

For reasons, she couldn't yet unveil, she had put the snake fork on the first place of the upmost shelf. And later, she had found a new place for the fork he had used. One made from the ivory horn of a unicorn.

The sun outside the windows wandered from the East to the South.

Still no customers.

Amanda of the Hidden Unknown stopped her rocking chair. The swinging only made her more anxious. She'd rather inspect the new fork. Or, rather, go and find out what was going on outside.

She turned to the door and pushed it open with her generous hip. The cobbled street was empty, the quickly put up houses of western town all around had neither windows nor curtains. Doors stood open. Dust heaps in every corner. A ghost town. Dry wind blew in her face.

She stepped back and let the door fall close.

Sometimes that happened. She made a triangular sign with her hands towards the door, to move that entrance to another, more vivid time of that city.

Then, she pushed the door open, using her shoulder.

Cold snowflakes blew straight into her face. Everything was white, and she shielded her eyes with her hands. In the snowstorm she couldn't make out any houses or living beings all around.

She stepped back and let the door fall close. She moved her hands and drew a second triangle pattern into the air. This door had to be moved as well. Maybe someplace warmer.

When was the last time, that she saw two empty places, lost places, when she had stepped out of the front door of her house?

Amanda couldn't remember. On normal days she stayed in, or left through the back door down the hall between her kitchen, the back-office and the stairs, leading up to her private rooms. Through the back door she also went to her gardens and the community living near her. Similar businesses with doors to various places, selling adventurer gear, books, herbs, knowledge, furniture and what not.

Her older sister ran the herbs shop.

The family business she inherited from their parents. Her tea shop was an abnormality. Had been one from the beginning, like she herself. Two daughters were wrong. One daughter and one son were expected. The daughter to take over the family business and the son to change the world of the humans.

Amanda firmly pressed her lips together and pushed past the cold in her stomach and the awful feeling of voice-lessness in her throat. She had value. Just not for the community. She still tried, by inventing a new business.

She sighted and pushed the bad feelings away as much as possible.

She had to solve the problem of lacking customers.

»Please, God of the Hidden and Goodness of the Unknown, let there be a prosperous city on the other side«, said Amanda with her suddenly sore throat and kicked the front door open with one foot.

The door banged against the wall of her house. She had used more force than necessary.

Amanda stepped forward and looked around.

No wind blew. No snow fell. It was sunny, warm and right before her feet, on the ground flowered tulips and daisies. A bit to the left she saw a forest and to the right was a lake.

No living being in sight. No house, no farm, nothing.

»What's wrong today?«, asked Amanda of the Unknown Hidden.

Silence answered.

Neither did the branches rustle, nor did the water splash or move in any direction. It felt like she stood in an image. A frozen version of nature. Lovely, but frozen.

She bent down to sniff at the flowers. No scent.

She pulled the door from the wall, stepped back and closed it.

That was worse than she had expected.

Just for the sake of tradition, she sealed that door as well, thinking of a place where people lived to reopen the door later.

Amanda left the room with her cup collection, walked straight past her plates, down the hall and into her back-office where she kept her books.

Stale air greeted her. She opened the two windows at the outer wall to let in fresh air. Yarrock blew a small flame from his nest in the corner.

He appreciated fresh air.

She smiled.

Outside she heard wind rustle, and children sing the lunch song. At least in that direction everything seemed normal.

Amanda of the Hidden Unknown turned to her desk on the one side wall.

Stacks of inventory books laid on the table. Usually she put them away after cataloging the latest additions, but yesterday she had been too tired to do it. She started to put away the books and stopped. There was no story under her entry of the greenish snake fork. Dread seemed to seep from the page. With a loud thumb she closed the book. With her lips pressed together she put the book away as well.

Finally, only her pen and the book for stories about her business remained. Next to them laid the three-headed snake knife the adventurer left with the dirty dishes.

She tenderly caressed the surface of the handle. Each scale was distinct.

A bird flew past her window.

Amanda blinked.

She had work to do. She could marvel at the knife liter.

She pulled her chair from under the table and sat down.

With green ink on the yellowish paper, she noted the three different worlds she had looked at, minutes ago. All, for the lack of better description, feeling empty. Not like any place someone lived. Describing the places made her shiver harder than she had, when the icy snowstorm blew straight in her face.

Each world had felt, as if mankind and magic, life and death had just decided to leave Earth from one day to the next. Or as if they had never been there. But where did everything go? And why on no notice at all, for her to prepare to follow and set up new doors?

Not that it mattered to Amanda. To her, and the community outside the open window, only her business success mattered. And a day without customers meant, she didn't get new inventory and therefore no new made-up stories of why items fit together. In the long run, she would be thrown out of the community if she wasn't successful. Especially, with her being the unwanted, second daughter already.

Obviously her God and Goodness hadn't seen fit to listen to her prayer and help. Therefore, she had to find a way by herself.

»Didn't you just forget me?«, asked a high-pitched, small voice.

Her companion and best friend, a fairy that rarely talked with her, flew down from her fairy house that appeared wherever she liked to live for the moment. Usually, Amanda's back-office but sometimes one of the other rooms.

»No, of course not, dear Princess«, said Amanda. »I would never forget you, your Highness. I just thought, the problem of lacking customers might be too far below your interests. Please excuse my false assumptions.«

The fairy flew down and sat on her shoulder.

Amanda grinned. She leaned back in her chair and relaxed a bit. Whenever the Princess sat on her shoulder everything was alright. The Princess loved being treated overly respectful.

»I would suggest«, said Amanda and stopped. She didn't have a plan yet, but she needed one, so she made it up, »to visit the business club and see, if others have similar issues.«

Princess sneezed at that. Obviously she disapproved the plan.

»I know you hate the other business owners. All women, all overly self-confident and no one treats you right«, said Amanda. »Nonetheless, research is necessary. Will you consider coming along, or are there issues that hinder your attendance?«

The banter with the fairy made her smile and eased the strange feeling sitting behind her neck a bit more. It felt as if somebody or something was watching every step of her, waiting for her to make a mistake. Like that strange adventurer was still here.

He had left yesterday. Hadn't he?

She had been so tired, and it had been late. He had promised to leave the dirty dishes on the table and close the door when he left. The dishes had been there this morning. The door had been closed. The adventurer had been gone.

»You left that thief alone?«, asked Princess and left the place on Amanda's shoulder. »Look!«

The princess pointed to a list hovering at the wall.

»I've told you time and again not to ever let a customer sit alone. And now I have to learn you missed the first rule?«

Princess tsk-tsked.

»I hope you followed the others, at least.«

Amanda felt her cheeks turn hot. She was not a child and no matter how much she liked the fairy, she wouldn't let herself be treated like a minor. She was a grown-up. Hundreds of years older than the fairy.

»Your stupid list is blocking valuable wall space for my bookkeeping. I'm not your child to chew out. And it's my business to let a trustworthy customer drink his tea on his own. Besides«, Amanda stopped and took in a deep breath, »the magic inherent in cherry tea makes everybody unable to steal anything. You know my older sister wouldn't ever make an error with that. So no risks involved.«

The fairy yawned and pointed to the last pint on the list.

»Don't accept gifts from strangers«, read Amanda out loud. »And if I do? Who will hinder me?«

She felt defensive. She remembered the small knife, that had laid on the dirty dish this morning. Another green snake with three heads. Only that, different from the fork, those heads were snuggled together at the top of the edge of the blade. Was that a gift? Or did the adventurer just forget it? Surely he would come back to fetch it. Besides, she had gotten gifts from customers before. None ever turned away the customers.

She looked at the knife she had laid on her desk, before she started to bake.

Well, none had ever been an item she didn't collect, like this little knife.

»I'm going to attend my new enthronement ceremony«, said the Princess and vanished, together with her house, from the back-office.

Amanda stayed behind. Kicked the desk and stared at the list, still on the wall. That's when she hated the fairy. Maybe she should allow her little dragon to roast and eat the flattery being. Yarrock would be very happy. But that would mean to lose her friend.

Yarrock blew a small flame from his nest.

Amanda got out of her chair, walked over and keeled down next to the nest.

»What's up Yarrock?«, asked Amanda, »do you think it is wrong to keep the knife?«

Amanda stroked the scaled back of her pet. Yarrock was to small too talk. In a few decades he might start, or so said the dragon hatchling book she had read.

»You know. The knife and the fork are of the same color as your scales«, said Amanda. »They even feel the same. Might be relatives of…«

Yarrock blew a flame in her direction, barely missing her.

Amanda fell on her back. The long skirts entangled between her legs.

»Stop that!«, said Amanda of the Hidden Unknown.

Yarrock didn't hide in his nest. Instead, he looked her straight in her face. His yellow eyes unblinking.

»Show me the knife.«

Amanda looked around. There was no one to speak to her. She looked to the shelf where Princess' house had been this morning. The spot was empty. Her friend had moved her house to another room.

»Show me the knife«, said the void again.

It seemed to be in her head.

Amanda concentrated. Could it be, that her God or Goodness had finally listened to her prayer and wanted to help? Not really. They could see everything if they wanted to.

»Who are you?«, asked Amanda and entangled her skirts from her ankles. She came up to her knees and patted the front of her dress down. The frills at the hem looked a bit sad, but a round of ironing could change that.

»Yarrock«, said the voice in her head.

Amanda stared at her dragon. A mind-speaking dragon?

Her day wasn't going to become easier.

At least she didn't have to search for the source any longer.

»The knife? Sure, come up on my arms«, said Amanda.

Yarrock climbed her dress.

The tissue ripped under his pointed, sharp claws. Something she had forgotten. Now it was too late. He curled around her neck until his eyes were level and next to hers.

Amanda walked back to the table and picked up the knife with the distinct scales. It was still green but seemed to glow from inside now.

»He cut you from the world«, said Yarrock. »That's the mythical knife.« He laid his head on her shoulder and closed his eyes.

Great.

Now she had a mind-speaking dragon, a mythical knife and no more doors into the human world. Could anything be worse?

Someone thundered against her back-door.

Amanda jumped.

Things obviously could get worse.

She hid the knife in a small pocket of her dress, left the sleeping dragon where he was and ran for the door. When she pulled it open, nobody was there. Maybe the children playing games. She had to get her nerves back under control, sort everything she knew and do something.

Amanda breathed in the fresh air. The taste of roasted potatoes hung in it and her stomach rumbled. There were so many cakes inside, and she hadn't eaten breakfast. Roasted potatoes sounded great for a pause and to think.

She made a step forward and hit an invisible wall.

»As I said. Cut off«, said Yarrock's voice in her head.

»How do I connect again?«, asked Amanda. Now her name was really true. Cut off from everything she finally was hidden and unknown to all, not only to the unbelieving humans.

She leaned against the wall. What did she know about the magic she used? Her mother had shown her the triangle pattern to draw into the air. A low level spell to create doors into the human world. Aside from that, her house was firmly built in the community she could see through the open door but not reach. She hadn't built it. Others have. Forgotten others. When she set up her shop, she had first renovated with her bare hands. Sometimes her sister had helped, giving her a herb to facilitate a task. If there were old spells in the house, she never felt them and her mother, coming once for the opening party, never mentioned them.

»Would it help to throw the knife out of the door?«, asked Amanda.

Throwing things away was a good cure to most of her problems. Cake too long in the oven? Throw it into the rubbish bin. Dirty dishes? Wash the dirt away. Dust or Snow on the floor behind the front door? Use the brush and brush it back out. Maybe the knife worked the same way?

She pulled it out from her pocket, aimed at the open door and threw.

The knife flew and vanished at the door.

Amanda didn't see it land outside on the brown, beaten path.

»Uhm.«

She tried to move her foot out of the door. The invisible wall was gone. As was the knife.

Amanda smiled, turned around and ran for the front door to see if the customers were back. She stood in the middle of the room and waited.

And waited.

No customer opened the door.

Her stomach rumbled. She was starving. Yarrock was heavy on her shoulders. But first she wanted to solve that problem. She had solved the problem at her back door. Hadn't she?

»No. You haven't«, said Yarrock's voice in her head. »You destroyed the barrier at the back door. The one cutting you from your community. You haven't repaired the front door.«

Amanda rolled her eyes. Why did everyone has to talk in riddles? Magic made them odd. That's why she loved her customers. Humans didn't make riddles out of each of their words.

»Where can I get the knife back to cut the wrong things from my front door?«, asked Amanda.

»You can't«, said Yarrock and wiggled on her shoulders. He put one paw over his face, and hid himself. »Use the other way.«

Then she heard a low snore.

Yarrock couldn't just go to sleep with that.

Amanda shook him.

No reaction. The dragon didn't move or react, just slept.

He's a baby, he needs the sleep, reminded Amanda herself. However, he had managed to talk to her mind, it might have used a lot of energy.

»Sleep well, little Yarrock«, whispered Amanda.

He had said use the other way, hadn't he? What was the other way? Obviously something she already had. But what?

Amanda turned around. The square tables with the red tablecloth stood unchanged. The walls were lined with her cups. The lower shelves were empty, waiting for future payments. The upper shelves were clean. All cups were there. She smiled. She loved them all. But if throwing and losing the knife was any hint, she might have to give up one item of her collection.

Her precious collection.

And who cut her from her community and moved her doors into empty times?

Might have been the adventurer yesterday. He had paid with a fork similar to the knife and been her last customer.

The fork!

Amanda left the room and stepped into the one with her forks. Everything seemed normal. The sames square tables as in the room with her cups. About half of the shelves filled with silvery, or green forks. She even had a blue one, she once got from a man living at the ocean shore telling a fantastic story about mermaids and monster. She pushed the memory away and focused on the upmost shelf at the first place.

There sat the fork made from the snake with the three heads forming the tips. The same green as yesterday.

She pulled a chair from the nearest table. Held her skirts aside and climbed up. She reached for the fork. The scales were as distinct under her touch as they had been on the knife.

She grabbed the fork and hopped off the chair.

Now the fork glowed in a light green from inside. Like the knife before.

Should she just throw it out the front door, as she had done with the back door? Would that repair all her doors?

Amanda slowly walked back into the cups room and leaned against one of her tables. Every time she opened the front door she saw a different world. She knew there were dozens of doors. If she threw out the fork, that might repair one door, but what about the others? If she was cut off, there had to be a web or something that connected her before. Maybe throwing the knife didn't cut, but spin a new connection.

She traced the three heads with her fingertip. Scaly, cold and hard.

Amanda rubbed her nose. She could throw out the fork, or she could use it like eating a cake. Stitch into each world and pull the fork back. Would that do the trick?

»Yarrock?«, asked Amanda.

The dragon on her shoulder didn't react.

»Princess?«

Her fairy friend didn't appear. Probably still at her enthronement ceremony.

Well, she could give it a try. If it didn't work, she could still throw the fork.

Amanda pushed off the table and walked to the door. She pushed it open with her generous hip, stuck out the fork into the silence and pulled it back in with closed eyes.

Clattering hooves and rumbling wagons mixed with shouting, male voices. The stench of horses blew in.

Amanda opened one eye. Then, the other.

There were men and horses walking past her door. The life was back. At least in front of this door.

She smiled, stepped back and let the door fall close.

Then, she steeled herself against the cold, in case her relocation sign hadn't worked and opened the door with her shoulder.

Cold snowflakes blew in.

Her relocation hadn't worked.

Nonetheless, she stuck out the fork and pulled it back in. Together with a small heap of snow, growing rapidly at the floor.

Amanda pushed the door closed. She could see nothing in the snow storm. Hopefully it had worked here as well.

She rubbed her arms and kicked the snow away, and off her skirts.

Now, to the last door. The fork in her hand still glowed faintly.

Before Amanda could kick the door open, it was pulled open from outside.

»Finally made it«, said a voice. »You're the tea shop, right?«

Amanda nodded, pushed the fork in her skirt pocket and stepped back.

»Welcome to the Tea Shop of the Hidden Unknown«, said Amanda and smiled. Here was her first customer of the day. A man covered in snow stepped in and pulled the door close.

She would reattach the other worlds later, after serving the first piece of one cake. And she would sit with the customer and eat a piece herself. The rumbling of her stomach was louder than before. Maybe she would use the porcelain cup with the blue roses as well and make herself a cup of hot chocolate to warm up.

The man stomped down the snow from his clothes and pulled open his jacket.

»Can I have a cup of cherry tea?«, asked the man.

»Of course«, said Amanda of the Hidden Unknown. »Choose your cup and plate. I'll cook the water.«

She rushed past her rocking chair, down the hall into the kitchen. She didn't understand what had happened, but was happy, she had a customer again.

Amanda smiled and stroked over the scaly body of her little baby dragon. »Thanks to you help«, she whispered and then reached for the water.

THE END

Excerpt:
Sweet Depths

"You bought those nasty, environment destroying chocolate lenses again?!" Ramona felt the rage pulse through her veins. They had a spaceship credit to pay down and her partner knew nothing better than throwing all his Christmas salary towards the sweets shop. She paced up and down through the room, searching her thoughts for a solution. Being late with the next payment rate meant the bank would sent their space ship to the next auction to get as much as possible to cover up for the unpaid costs.

Ramona felt hot and cold the same time. Sweat started to pearl over her forehead and whetted her shirt on the back. Losing her ship would be the end of their dream of independence. Freedom from the empire which decided who worked what. The last months had been slow with transportation orders, but everyone had to start somewhere. She had worked hard for a good reputation as independent transport ship captain. Teckkars had joined the work force again to pay the credit while she fulfilled the orders alone until he could quit again. At least she had decided to do so.

"Have you forgotten why you are working there? To pay down the credit faster", Ramona remembered her husband.

"Well then, darling", Ramona stopped in front of Teckkars who still ate those dreaded chocolate lenses, which, how she had to remind her to avoid eating some of them too, not only ruined the earth climate and forced people to live in space but was now in charge of ruining her freedom too. "I will set up a household plan and give you a monthly budget for sweets. All other money is administrated by me and only me."

Ramona paused, hoping he wouldn't protest but expected a fiery and fierce refusal. It didn't came. Surprised and unsure if she liked the outcome of this discussion, she left the room to change the authority of his money account to hers.

She would implement a thoughtful budget plan. Ra-

mona smiled at the screen. She preferred being in control.
The money she withdraws from Teckkars account had
nothing to do with that feeling of superiority, she reas-
sured herself.

25

∿∿⊗∿∿

Excerpt end of: Sweet Depths

More books

Sherik'anaan steps back. She merges with the background. As good as she can. Conjuring food for the whole party? A bad idea.

People stare at her and her generous curves. Curves she can't hex away.

Questions start: "So what's the trick, Sherik'anaan?" - "How did you do it?" Time to leave. Or give it a try.

Run along with this fantasy short story and find out if Sherik'anaan, the mage, survives the crowd.

The True Mage survives

Fairy-tales come true. Or rather their items make appearances. To those who search for them.

Frauke applies for a new job as software developer. After staying at home for six years, with her children. Can she convince the people she knows enough?

Nervous she stands in the ladies room. In front of the mirror. She thinks about her favorite fairy-tale of snow-white. What if the magic mirror really existed? Could it tell her about her job chances?

Then, her reflection winks back to her. Frauke thinks herself crazy.

A job interview, a voice talking, nobody can her beside her and a mirror that winks back at her. Join in on this fantastical job interview.

Fantasy

Beaten Path in the Mist
Vampire Hunting with the Tiger Eye
Marlene's New Monster
Remorse of the Mermaid
Wipe off the Dust
The Book Burning

Stars Flying into Philosophy
Red: #890000
The True Mage Survives
The Flower on the Mountain Top
The speaking Mirror
The Fork with the Scales

Romance

World Cup and Pink Ropes
An Invitation to a Wedding
Corrupted Food Storage
Dance to your Love
Fighting the Cinnamon Guy
Forgotten Communications

The Magic Book
Love against all Rules
Love as a Christmas Present
The Griffin's Wedding Ring
Crossroads with Half the Information (Collection)

Science Fiction

Abandonned Time Travel
Alien Visit
Coloring an Apple
Corrupted Food Storage
Dicovery (Novel)
Red: #890000
Served like red Wine
Shards of her Life

Support Refused
Sweet Depths
The Water Theft
Lottery Win: The Third Set of Doors
Human Interactions Preferred
Intertwined Fate